In loving memory

First published in Great Britain in 2012 by
Piccadilly Press Ltd, 5 Castle Road, London NW1 8PR
www.piccadillypress.co.uk

Text and illustration copyright © Tony Maddox, 2012

Designed by Simon Davis
Printed and bound in China by WKT
Colour reproduction by Dot Gradations

ISBN: 978 1 84812 090 7 (paperback)

1 3 5 7 9 10 8 6 4 2

Well Done, Little Croc!

Tony Maddox

Piccadilly Press • London

Little Croc loved playing games
with his friends . . .

but, although he tried his hardest, he just wasn't as good as the others.

Giraffe was good at heading the ball
because he was so tall,

and Monkey was good at catching the ball
because she could jump so high,

and Cheetah was good at chasing the ball
because he could run so fast.

"It's no use," Little Croc said
to Mummy Croc.

"I can't run fast with my short crocodile legs . . .

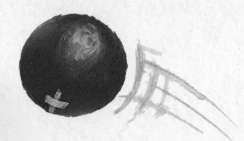

and I can't jump
high with my long
crocodile tail...

and I can't catch
the ball because
my crocodile nose
gets in the way."

Mummy Croc did her best to comfort him.

"Everyone is good at something," she said.

"You just haven't found what you're good at yet!"

"I don't think I'll ever be good at anything!"

Little Croc said with a sigh.

Little Croc went and sat by the river.

"Come and play!" called Bird.

"I don't want to!" Little Croc replied grumpily,
as he thumped his tail crossly.

It seemed as if he had
been there for hours
when something splashed into
the water in front of him.
It was the ball!

The animals rushed over, but it was too late.
The ball was already floating away down the river!

"We'll never get it
back now!" they cried.

"I'll get it!" Little Croc shouted and dived into the river.

He swam as fast as he could
until finally he reached the ball,
just as it was about to go
over the waterfall.

Holding it firmly,
he began to make
the long swim back,
when he noticed
something
lying on the rock.

It was Mr Snuggles,
Monkey's lost
teddy bear!

Then he noticed something
else, stuck in the middle
of the reeds.

It was Cheetah's lost
toy boat!

And further on, caught
on a fallen branch of a tree,
was Giraffe's missing straw hat!

"Monkey and Cheetah and Giraffe will be really pleased that I've found their things!" thought Little Croc as he reached the bank.

And they were!

"My hat!" cried Giraffe.

"My toy boat!" cried Cheetah.

"Mr Snuggles!" cried Monkey.

"What a great surprise!" they all said.

"Well done, Little Croc!"

They were so delighted, they gave
Little Croc a special medal made from
an old jam pot lid and some red ribbon.
"For being the Best Finder of Lost Things,"
they said.

Proudly, Little Croc hurried home to show Mummy Croc.

"I found out what I'm best at!" he cried.

"I swam very fast and rescued the ball,

and I found things my friends had lost."

Little Croc was so excited.

"Well done, Little Croc!"
said Mummy Croc proudly.
"You see, you are good at lots
of things after all."
And she gave him a great
big crocodile hug.